STERLING CHILDREN'S BOOKS
New York

An Imprint of Sterling Publishing
387 Park Avenue South
New York, NY 10016

ISBN 978-1-4027-8337-1

Library of Congress Cataloging-in-Publication Data Available

Distributed in Canada by Sterling Publishing
c/o Canadian Manda Group, 165 Dufferin Street
Toronto, Ontario, Canada M6K 3H6
Distributed in the United Kingdom by GMC Distribution Services
Castle Place, 166 High Street, Lewes, East Sussex, England BN7 1XU
Distributed in Australia by Capricorn Link (Australia) Pty. Ltd.
P.O. Box 704, Windsor, NSW 2756, Australia

For information about custom editions, special sales, and premium and corporate
purchases, please contact Sterling Special Sales at 800-805-5489
or specialsales@sterlingpublishing.com.

Printed in China
Lot #:
2 4 6 8 10 9 7 5 3
09/13

www.sterlingpublishing.com/kids

SILVER PENNY STORIES

Little Red Riding Hood

Told by Deanna McFadden

Illustrated by Scott Wakefield

Once upon a time there was
a little girl who loved her
grandmother. Her grandmother also
loved her very much and made her
a red velvet cloak with a hood. The
little girl became known as Little Red
Riding Hood.

One day, Little Red Riding Hood set out to visit her grandmother, who was not feeling well.

"Don't stray from the path on your way!" her mother said, handing her a basket of food for Grandmother.

The path took Little Red Riding Hood deep into the woods, where she met a big, bad wolf.

"Where are you going, Little Red Riding Hood?" he asked her with false kindness.

"I'm on my way to Grandmother's house," she answered. "She's not feeling well."

"Where is Grandmother's house?" the wolf asked.

"You must have seen it," Little Red Riding Hood said. "It's right next to the three tall oak trees."

The wolf walked beside Little Red Riding Hood. They came to a field full of beautiful flowers. "Why don't you pick some for Grandmother?" he suggested.

Little Red Riding Hood stepped off the path into the field of flowers. She picked and picked. She forgot all about her grandmother.

Meanwhile, the wolf raced to Grandmother's house.

"Who's there?" Grandmother called.

The wolf said, "It's Little Red Riding Hood. I've brought food to help you feel better."

"Come right in, dear," Grandmother said. "The door is open."

The weak woman was no match for the big, bad wolf. He swallowed her right up! Then, he put on her nightcap and glasses and climbed into her bed.

Little Red Riding Hood's arms were full of flowers when she remembered she was supposed to visit her grandmother. She stepped back onto the path and ran the rest of the way.

When Little Red Riding Hood arrived at Grandmother's house, she was surprised to find the front door open.

"Hello!" she called as she stepped through the door. "Grandmother?"

She saw her grandmother lying in bed with her cap pulled down over her face.

"Grandmother, what big ears you have!" said Little Red Riding Hood.

"The better to hear you with," the wolf said.

"And what big eyes you have!" said Little Red Riding Hood.

"The better to see you with," the wolf replied.

"And what big hands you have!"
said Little Red Riding Hood.

"The better to hug you with,"
the wolf declared.

"And what big teeth you have!" said Little Red Riding Hood.

"The better to eat you with!" the wolf growled.

With that, the big, bad wolf leaped out of the bed and gobbled up Little Red Riding Hood! The wolf was so full, he fell asleep right away, snoring very loudly.

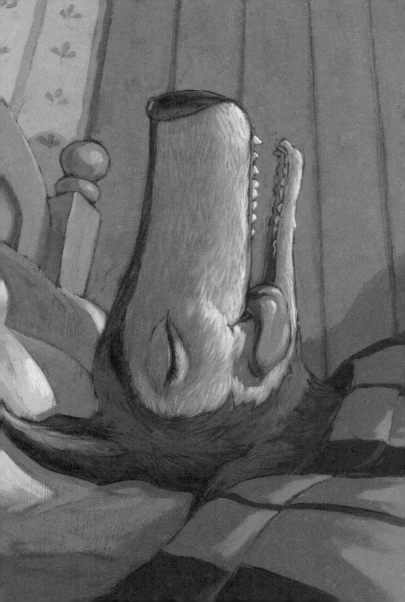

A local hunter walked by and heard
the noise from the terrible snoring.

"Grandmother is never that loud.
Something strange is going on,"
he said to himself.

He crept into the house and found
the wolf asleep on the bed.

He looked around for Grandmother. But he only found Little Red Riding Hood's basket and a piece of her red cloak.

The wolf must have eaten them, the hunter thought.

The hunter was very brave. He walked up to the sleeping wolf and pulled Little Red Riding Hood right out of its belly.

"Oh, thank you for getting me out of there. It was so dark and scary!" she said.

The hunter pulled Grandmother out next.

The wolf saw the hunter pick up his sharp ax. Next, he saw Grandmother and Little Red Riding Hood.

Frightened, the wolf quickly stumbled out of the house. He knew never to bother Grandmother again.

Grandmother thanked the hunter for saving their lives. Then, they all sat down to a fine meal.

As Little Red Riding Hood watched the big, bad wolf run away, she said, "I will never again stray from the path on my way to Grandmother's house."